D0960896

To Mr. Warburton,
who makes me itch

This book is set in Century 725/Monotype; Grilled Cheese BTN/Fontbros; Typography of Coop, Fink,
Neutraface/House Industries

Printed in Malaysia
Reinforced binding

First Edition, October 2009
FAC-029191-16355
20 19 18 17 16 15 14 13

Library of Congress Cataloging-in-Publication Data on file.
ISBN: 978-1-4231-1411-6

Visit www.hyperionbooksforchildren.com and www.pigeonpresents.com

# Make Me Sneeze!

An ELEPHANT & PIGGIE Book

By Mo Willems

Hyperion Books for Children / *New York*
AN IMPRINT OF DISNEY BOOK GROUP

Gerald!

I want— **a a a**

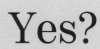

SNIFF!

19

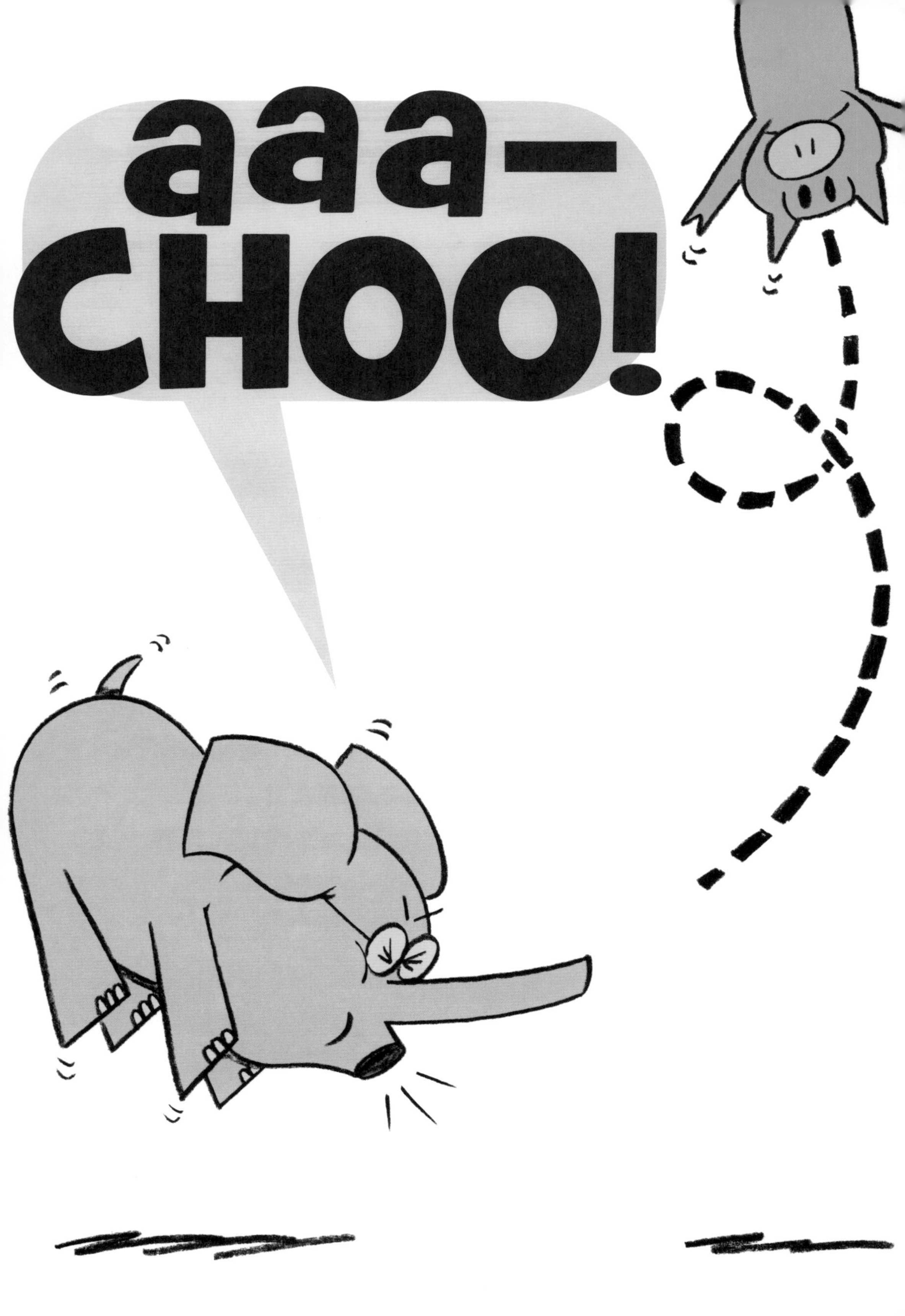
aaa-
CHOO!

But, if pigs *do* make
me sneeze...

25

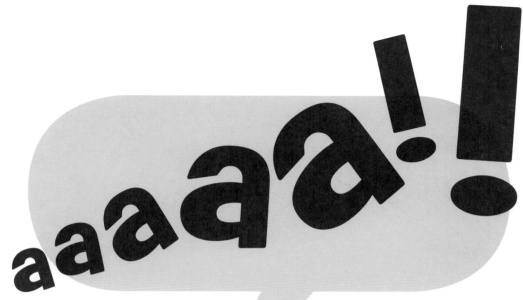

Good-bye.

Gerald . . .

SNIFF!

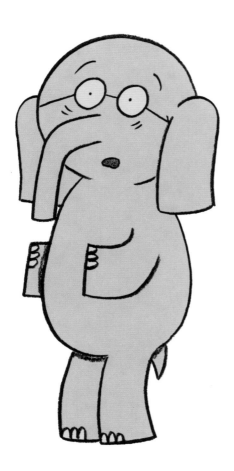

And Piggie
is a pig!

45

THUD!

51

54

# Great news!

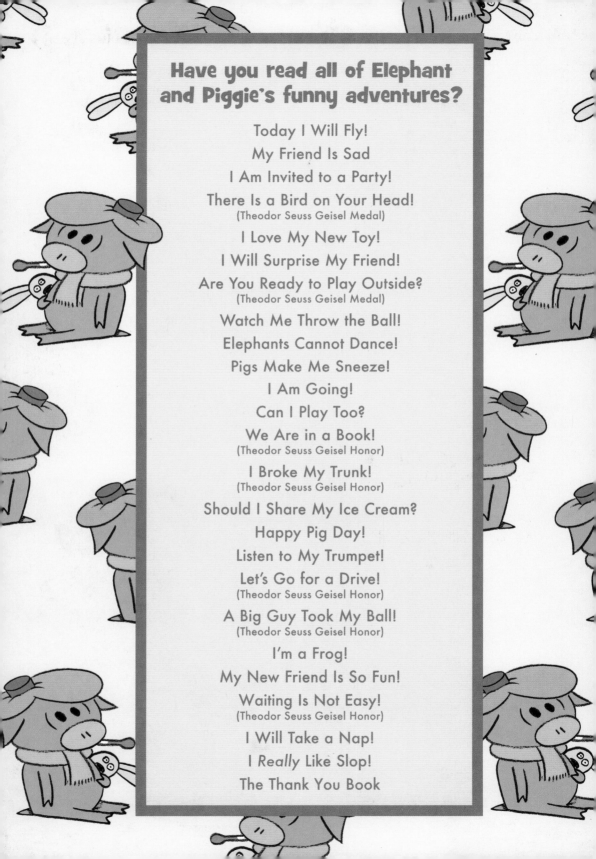

# Have you read all of Elephant and Piggie's funny adventures?